I0663305

Mr. Prohartchin

Poverty, Pride,
and the Tragic Irony of a Miser's Life

A Modern Translation

Adapted for the Contemporary Reader

Fyodor Dostoevsky

Translated by Tim Zengerink

© Copyright 2025
All rights reserved.

It is not legal to reproduce, duplicate, or transmit any part of this document in either electronic means or in printed format. Recording of this publication is strictly prohibited and any storage of this document is not allowed unless with written permission from the publisher except for the use of brief quotations in a book review.

This book contains works of fiction. Any resemblance to persons living or dead, or places, events, or locations is purely coincidental.

Table of Contents

Preface - Message to the Reader

What If You Could Help Rebuild the Greatest Library in Human History?

Thousands of years ago, the Library of Alexandria stood as the crown jewel of human achievement — a sanctuary where the collected wisdom of every known civilization was gathered, preserved, and shared freely.

And then, it was lost.

Through fire, conquest, and the slow erosion of time, humanity lost not just books — but ideas, dreams, discoveries, and stories that could have changed the world forever.

Today, the Library of Alexandria lives again — and you are invited to be a part of its restoration.

Our mission is simple yet profound:

To rebuild the greatest library the world has ever known, and to translate all timeless works into every language and dialect, so that no seeker of knowledge is ever left behind again.

By joining our movement to rebuild the modern Library of Alexandria, you become part of an unprecedented mission:

1

Unlimited Access to the Greatest Audiobooks & eBooks Ever Written:

Instantly explore thousands of legendary works—Plato, Shakespeare, Jane Austen, Leo Tolstoy, and countless more. All instantly available to read or listen, placing a complete literary universe at your fingertips.

Beautiful Paperback & Deluxe Editions at Printing Cost

Own any title as an elegant paperback, deluxe hardcover, or stunning collectible boxset—offered to you at true printing cost, delivered straight to your door. Build your personal Library of Alexandria, crafted for beauty, built for durability, and worthy of proud display.

Fresh Translations for Modern Readers—in Every Language & Dialect

Enjoy timeless masterpieces reimagined in clear, contemporary language—no more outdated phrases or obscure references. Alongside the original versions, we're tirelessly translating these classics into every language and dialect imaginable, ensuring accessibility and understanding across cultures and generations.

Join a Global Renaissance of Literature & Knowledge

You directly support expanding our library, publishing deluxe editions at true cost, translating works into all global languages, and bringing humanity's greatest stories to people everywhere. By joining today, you're not just preserving a legacy of masterpieces; you set in motion a powerful wave of literary accessibility.

Become a Torchbearer of Knowledge.

Join us for free now at **LibraryofAlexandria.com**

Together, we will ensure that the light of human wisdom never fades again.

With gratitude and a shared love of knowledge,

The Modern Library of Alexandria Team

Visit:

www.libraryofalexandria.com

Or scan the code below:

Introduction

The Hidden Tragedy of a Life
Lived in Fear and Pride

Fyodor Dostoevsky's Mr. Prohartchin, first published in 1846, is a short but remarkably poignant study in psychological realism and social irony. Written during the early years of his literary career, the story is often overlooked compared to his later, more famous works. Yet it stands as a powerful foreshadowing of the themes Dostoevsky would spend a lifetime exploring: alienation, the burden of poverty, the complexity of pride, and the ways individuals suffer silently in the margins of society. With precise observational detail and a touch of grim humor, Mr. Prohartchin gives voice to the inner torment of a man who lives on the edge of destitution—not because he has no money, but because he is too frightened, too proud, and too ashamed to spend what he has.

The story revolves around the titular character, Mumy Prohartchin, a timid, reclusive, and elderly man who boards in a shared lodging house. He is mocked and pitied by his fellow tenants, who suspect he may be hiding a small fortune despite living in almost comical poverty. He hoards his meager meals, shivers through winter without a proper coat, and obsesses over minute savings. He becomes increasingly withdrawn and neurotic, retreating into a world of paranoia and defensive outbursts. When he dies suddenly, his possessions are searched—and indeed, money is found, hidden away in bundles, untouched. The final irony lands with a cruel sting: Mr. Prohartchin could have lived in modest comfort, but his fear of judgment, his social anxiety, and his internalized shame denied him even the simplest pleasures of life.

Dostoevsky's treatment of Mr. Prohartchin is neither sentimental nor mocking. The tone is one of restrained empathy—a recognition that beneath the absurdities of the man's behavior lies a profound moral and emotional struggle. He is not merely a miser, but a tragic figure: someone crushed by the weight of social perception, institutional neglect, and the personal terror of inadequacy. His life is a silent protest against vulnerability, and in the end, it is that silence that seals his fate.

Shame, Solitude, and the Delusions of the Poor

In Mr. Prohartchin, Dostoevsky explores poverty not only as an economic condition but as a psychological state. The protagonist does not live poorly because he has to—he lives poorly because he cannot bear the thought of exposure. He is consumed by a desire to appear respectable and unremarkable, even as his behavior becomes increasingly bizarre and contradictory. His hoarding is not an expression of greed but of fear: fear of illness, of destitution, of becoming dependent on others. But more than anything, it is a fear of being seen as weak.

This fear isolates him. Though surrounded by other tenants, Mr. Prohartchin is profoundly alone. He does not trust his neighbors, nor do they trust him. Their relationship is defined by rumor, annoyance, and suspicion. And yet, Dostoevsky allows us to see that the judgment Mr. Prohartchin so dreads is largely internal. He imagines humiliation, constructs insults in his mind, and interprets every conversation as a potential threat to his dignity. In doing so, he creates the very alienation he fears most.

Herein lies the story's tragic irony: Mr. Prohartchin dies in obscurity, surrounded by neighbors who feel neither affection nor hatred for him, only mild curiosity and a touch of ridicule. When his hoarded money is found, it confirms their suspicions but inspires no admiration. There is no redemption, no revelation—only a confirmation of life wasted on imagined shame. And yet, Dostoevsky suggests that Mr. Prohartchin is not a monster or a madman. He is one of us. He is what happens when vulnerability is met with scorn, and when the poor are left to suffer behind the mask of pride.

This modern translation retains the subtle shifts in tone, from humor to pathos, that characterize Dostoevsky's early prose, while modernizing the language to make it emotionally accessible to today's reader. The story's insights into human behavior, economic insecurity, and social invisibility remain as urgent now as they were in 19th-century Russia.

In conclusion, Mr. Prohartchin is a masterclass in literary understatement. It offers no grand epiphany, no sweeping moral. Instead, it delivers something rarer: a quiet, devastating look at how fear, pride, and shame can conspire to make a life smaller than it needs to be. In the figure of the anxious miser, Dostoevsky captures the universal pain of being unseen and misunderstood—and offers a gentle, if haunting, reminder of the cost of withholding compassion.

A story

In the smallest and most modest corner of Ustinya Fyodorovna's apartment lived Semyon Ivanovitch Prohartchin, a kind-hearted elderly man who never drank. Since Mr. Prohartchin held a very low-ranking position at work and earned a salary that matched his humble status, Ustinya Fyodorovna could only charge him five roubles a month for rent. Some people claimed she had her own reasons for keeping him as a tenant, but whatever those reasons might have been, it was clear that Mr. Prohartchin became her favorite lodger. This favoritism, of course, was entirely honorable and proper.

It's worth noting that Ustinya Fyodorovna, a respectable woman with a particular love for meat and coffee—making it hard for her to observe fasting days—rented rooms to several other boarders. These tenants paid her twice what Semyon Ivanovitch did, yet they were far from her favorites. Most of them were loud and argumentative, often mocking her domestic habits and vulnerability. If it hadn't been for the money they brought in, she would have gladly avoided their company and refused to rent to them altogether. In contrast, Semyon Ivanovitch had earned her preference ever since a former tenant, a retired or possibly dismissed clerk with a heavy drinking problem, had passed away and been buried in Volkovo Cemetery.

That previous tenant, despite having only one eye and one leg—injuries he proudly attributed to his bravery—had somehow gained all of Ustinya Fyodorovna's affection. He had fully taken advantage of her kindness, living as her loyal companion and flattery-filled admirer. He might have continued to do so for years if he hadn't ultimately drunk himself to death in a pitiful manner. This tragic chapter of her life unfolded in her old apartment in Peski, where she had only three lodgers at the time. When she moved to a larger flat to expand her rental business and took in nearly a dozen new tenants, Semyon Ivanovitch was the only one from her earlier days who remained.

From the very beginning, there seemed to be tension between Mr. Prohartchin and the newer boarders. It's hard to say whether this was due to some flaws in his character or because of the others' behavior, but misunderstandings arose on both sides. Meanwhile, the new tenants all got along famously with each other. Many of them worked in the same office, and they often gambled away their earnings to one another in games like faro, preference, and bixe. They enjoyed spending time together, diving into lively discussions about lofty topics, which frequently ended in heated debates. Yet, despite these disagreements, they shared a camaraderie, free from lingering grudges or prejudices.

Among these tenants were several notable personalities. Mark Ivanovitch stood out as an intelligent and well-read man, while Oplevaniev and Prepolovenko were known for their friendly and modest natures. Zinovy Prokofyevitch dreamed of climbing the social ladder into aristocratic circles, and Okeanov, a copying clerk, had nearly surpassed Semyon Ivanovitch in popularity among the group. Another copying clerk, Sudbin, along with the down-to-earth Kantarev, rounded out the diverse group of characters. There were others as well, each adding to the vibrant, if occasionally chaotic, dynamic of the household.

In contrast, Semyon Ivanovitch remained somewhat of an outsider. While no one harbored ill will toward him, he never fully integrated into the group. From the beginning, his fellow tenants acknowledged his positive traits. Mark Ivanovitch, in particular, often defended him, declaring that Mr. Prohartchin was a good-natured and harmless man, though not exactly worldly or imaginative. He wasn't prone to flattery, and while he had his flaws, his unhappiness was largely attributed to his lack of imagination.

Physically, Mr. Prohartchin didn't make a strong impression, and his mannerisms didn't win him any favor with the more critical boarders. Still, his appearance didn't provoke outright ridicule. Mark Ivanovitch, who prided himself on his intelligence, described him as an elderly, respectable man who had long outgrown any romantic notions of life. In the end, if Semyon Ivanovitch struggled to connect with others, it seemed to be his own failing, born of his inability to navigate social interactions.

The first thing everyone noticed about Semyon Ivanovitch was his undeniable stinginess and extreme frugality. This was immediately apparent because he refused to lend anyone his teapot, not even for a moment. This was especially unfair since he rarely used it himself. Instead, he preferred drinking a homemade brew of wildflowers and medicinal herbs, which he always kept in ample supply. His eating habits were just as peculiar. Unlike the other lodgers, Semyon Ivanovitch never indulged in the full dinner that Ustinya Fyodorovna prepared daily for her boarders. That meal cost half a rouble, but Semyon Ivanovitch paid only twenty-five kopecks in small change and stuck rigidly to this amount. For his modest payment, he would take either a bowl of soup with a piece of pie or a small plate of beef. More often, though, he skipped both soup and beef, settling instead for simple fare like white bread with onion, curds, salted cucumber, or something similarly cheap. Only when he could no longer endure such a frugal diet would he opt for the half-rouble dinner.

The biographer must admit that it would have been preferable to avoid such mundane and unflattering details, which may offend readers who favor a more heroic or dignified style. However, these details reveal something unique about the character of Semyon Ivanovitch. The truth is that he wasn't nearly as poor as his habits might suggest. He could have afforded proper meals if he wanted them, but his peculiar choices stemmed from his frugality and excessive caution. As strange as it may seem, he acted this way without concern for what others thought of him, simply to satisfy his own odd whims. These tendencies will become clearer later in the story, but for now, we will avoid boring the reader by delving too deeply into every one of his eccentricities. For example, we will skip the amusing details about his wardrobe. In fact, if not for Ustinya Fyodorovna's testimony, we might not even mention that Semyon Ivanovitch almost never sent his linen to the wash. On the rare occasions he did, so much time would pass between washes that one could forget he owned linen at all.

According to Ustinya Fyodorovna, who had observed him closely, "Poor Semyon Ivanovitch, bless his soul, was such a dear but peculiar man. For twenty years, he lived quietly in his little corner, completely indifferent to what people thought of him. All his life, he managed without socks, handkerchiefs, or such things." She even claimed to have seen, thanks to the worn-out state of the screen dividing his corner, that the poor man sometimes lacked proper clothing altogether.

These were the stories that circulated after Semyon Ivanovitch's death. But during his lifetime, his peculiar habits often led to misunderstandings and arguments. One of the most frequent sources of conflict was his insistence on privacy. He couldn't stand anyone—no matter how friendly—poking around his corner, even if they happened to glance through a hole in the old screen. Semyon Ivanovitch was a reserved man, not easy to get along with, and often in poor health. He disliked unsolicited advice and had no patience for people who tried to assert themselves around him. If anyone dared to mock him or offer unwanted suggestions, he was quick to retaliate, shaming them with cutting words.

"You're nothing but a puppy, a fool with no business giving advice," he would snap. "Mind your own affairs! Better count the stitches in your own socks before you try meddling in mine!"

Semyon Ivanovitch was a simple man who never used formal language with anyone. He especially disliked it when someone, knowing his quirks, would tease him by asking questions, like what he kept in his small trunk. That trunk, which sat under his bed, was guarded as though it were a priceless treasure. Everyone knew it contained nothing but old rags, a couple of damaged boots, and other odds and ends, yet Semyon Ivanovitch valued it greatly. In fact, people had heard him complain about the trunk's old, though functional, lock and talk about buying a new, complicated German lock with a secret spring.

Once, Zinovy Prokofyevitch, in a careless moment, made an unkind joke, suggesting that Semyon Ivanovitch might be hoarding something in the trunk to leave behind for his descendants. This crude remark left everyone who overheard it stunned by the reaction it provoked. At first, Semyon Ivanovitch struggled to respond, muttering incoherent words in frustration. Eventually, his meaning became clear. He accused Zinovy of some past wrongdoing and predicted that Zinovy would never achieve his dream of entering high society. He went on to declare that Zinovy would end up being beaten by a tailor to whom he owed money.

"You're nothing but a puppy," Semyon Ivanovitch shouted angrily. "You dream of joining the hussars, but I tell you, you'll only embarrass yourself. And mark my words, when your superiors find out what you're really like, they'll make you a mere copying clerk! That's all you'll ever be, do you hear me, puppy?"

After delivering his tirade, Semyon Ivanovitch seemed to calm down. But five hours later, much to everyone's amazement, he started ranting about Zinovy Prokofyevitch again, first mumbling to himself and then addressing Zinovy directly. That evening, when Mark Ivanovitch and Prepolovenko were making tea and invited Okeanov to join them, Semyon Ivanovitch got out of bed and joined the group, contributing his fifteen or twenty kopecks as usual. Under the pretext of wanting tea, he launched into a lengthy explanation about his financial situation. He declared himself a poor man, emphasizing that he was only admitting this because the subject had come up. He explained that he had planned to borrow a rouble from Zinovy the day before but had decided against it to avoid giving the "puppy" something to brag about. He complained about his meager salary, which he said wasn't enough to buy proper food, and revealed that he sent five roubles every month to his sister-in-law in Tver to support her. Without his financial help, he claimed, she would die.

And if not for this obligation, he added, he would have bought himself a new suit long ago.

Semyon Ivanovitch rambled on, repeating himself over and over as if trying to convince his audience. Eventually, he became so muddled that he fell silent. However, three days later, long after everyone else had forgotten the incident, he suddenly added a final comment. He declared that if Zinovy Prokofyevitch ever did manage to join the hussars, he'd end up losing a leg in battle and coming back with a wooden leg. Zinovy would then beg Semyon Ivanovitch for food, but Semyon Ivanovitch vowed that he wouldn't give him anything or even acknowledge him.

This peculiar behavior fascinated and amused the other lodgers. Out of sheer curiosity, they decided to team up and probe Semyon Ivanovitch further. Since Semyon Ivanovitch had a habit of asking nosy questions about their lives, their interactions with him seemed to evolve naturally. Semyon Ivanovitch had a predictable way of joining conversations. Around tea time, he would quietly approach a group gathered for tea, hand over his twenty kopecks to join in, and behave in a friendly and reasonable manner. But the younger men, often exchanging mischievous glances, would take this as an opportunity to play tricks on him.

Their conversations would start innocently enough, but soon one of the more imaginative lodgers would spin a wild tale, full of absurd and unbelievable details. For instance, someone might claim that a high-ranking official had said married clerks were more reliable and likely to be promoted because marriage made them more stable. This would lead to the speaker declaring his own intentions to marry someone named Fevronya Prokofyevna for the sake of his career. Or they might suggest that clerks lacking refined manners should have their salaries docked so the funds could be used to hire a hall where they could learn to dance and cultivate gentlemanly qualities.

The group would pretend to take these stories seriously, asking questions, speculating about the consequences, and even feigning worry about how these imaginary policies might affect them. Even someone far less gullible than Semyon Ivanovitch might have been fooled by such a unanimous show of belief. But Semyon Ivanovitch, being slow to grasp new ideas, struggled to process these tales. He needed time to "chew over" and "digest" what he heard, often ending up confused or bewildered before finally making sense of it in his own peculiar way.

Semyon Ivanovitch began to show strange and unexpected traits that no one had noticed before. These changes led to gossip and speculation, which eventually reached his workplace, though with exaggerated details added along the way. What made it all more sensational was that Mr. Prohartchin, who had always been known for his calm and consistent demeanor, suddenly appeared uneasy and nervous. His expression became timid and suspicious, and he started walking quietly, as though listening and watching for something. To make things even more peculiar, he developed an obsession with uncovering the truth behind the rumors circulating about him. On two occasions, he even dared to approach Demid Vassilyevitch, his superior, to ask if these strange stories were true. Out of respect for Semyon Ivanovitch's reputation, we will not delve into the consequences of this bold move.

These changes made people view him as reclusive and indifferent to proper behavior. They also began to think of him as somewhat eccentric, and there was some truth to this assumption. It was observed more than once that he would sit at his desk as if frozen, his pen suspended mid-air, his mouth slightly open, looking more like the shadow of a person than a real one. Sometimes his vacant, wandering gaze would startle his coworkers. If someone accidentally locked eyes with him, they might become so unnerved that they would smudge their paperwork or write something completely inappropriate in an important document. His peculiar behavior frustrated and embarrassed those who valued proper etiquette.

The belief that Semyon Ivanovitch's mind was not quite right became undeniable one morning when news spread that he had frightened Demid Vassilyevitch himself. According to the story, Semyon Ivanovitch had behaved so oddly during an encounter in the corridor that his superior had to back away and leave. When Semyon Ivanovitch heard about this incident, he reacted immediately. He got up, carefully made his way between the chairs and desks, put on his overcoat, and left the office without saying a word. He disappeared for a while, leaving no sign of himself either at home or at work. Whether this was due to fear or some other impulse, no one could say.

It wouldn't be fair to attribute Semyon Ivanovitch's strange behavior entirely to eccentricity. However, it's important to note that he was an extremely private man, unaccustomed to social interaction. Before meeting his new housemates, he had lived a solitary and uneventful life. During the years he lived in Peski, he spent most of his time lying on his bed behind a screen, keeping to himself and rarely speaking to anyone. His old fellow lodgers were just as reclusive as he was. They also lived hidden behind screens for years, leading quiet, uneventful lives. Days and weeks passed in peaceful monotony, and everything around them remained the same. This tranquil way of life was so consistent that neither Semyon Ivanovitch nor Ustinya Fyodorovna could recall exactly when he had first moved in.

"It could be ten years, maybe twenty, or even twenty-five," Ustinya Fyodorovna would sometimes say to her newer tenants. "He's been with me all this time, the poor dear man."

Given this background, it was no surprise that Semyon Ivanovitch, being so unaccustomed to lively company, was deeply unsettled when, about a year earlier, his quiet existence was disrupted. The respectable and modest man suddenly found himself surrounded by a loud, boisterous group of a dozen young men—his new colleagues and housemates.Semyon Ivanovitch's sudden disappearance caused quite a commotion among the lodgers. For one thing, he was the landlady's favorite tenant. For another, his passport, which had been kept by Ustinya Fyodorovna, had somehow gone missing. This prompted the landlady to erupt into her usual fit of wailing and scolding. For two days, she berated the other lodgers, accusing them of driving Semyon Ivanovitch away as if he were some helpless chicken. On the third day, she demanded that they all go out and search for him, ordering them to bring him back, dead or alive.

That evening, Sudbin returned first with news. He claimed to have seen Semyon Ivanovitch at Tolkutchy Market and later in other places, including among a crowd watching a house on fire in Crooked Lane. However, despite following him closely, Sudbin had not dared to speak to him. Not long after, Okeanov and Kantarev arrived and confirmed Sudbin's account. They, too, had seen him and had followed him at a distance but hadn't mustered the courage to approach him. Both added that Semyon Ivanovitch appeared to be walking with a drunk vagrant.

By the time all the lodgers had gathered, they concluded that Semyon Ivanovitch couldn't have gone far and would likely return soon. Many of them admitted they had suspected he was spending time with this drunken vagabond, a man who had recently entered their lives. This vagrant was a shady character—both insolent and fawning—and had somehow ingratiated himself with Semyon Ivanovitch. About a week before Semyon Ivanovitch disappeared, this man had arrived in the company of Remnev, another tenant, and told an elaborate tale about his life. He claimed to have suffered for the cause of justice, having once served in a provincial office until an inspector came down on them.

According to his story, he was wrongfully dismissed due to his enemies' schemes. He said he had later come to Petersburg to plead his case before Porfiry Grigoryevitch and had briefly secured a position in a department, only to lose it again when the office was reorganized. He blamed his misfortunes on a combination of his own unsuitability for official work and the unjust treatment he received. This long and dramatic tale was punctuated by frequent embraces and kisses directed at his gloomy companion, Remnev.

After finishing his story, this man, who introduced himself as Zimoveykin, went on to charm everyone in the flat. He bowed to each person in turn, including Avdotya, the servant, and repeatedly called them his benefactors. He admitted to being a troublesome, foolish man and begged for their kindness. Later, he showed a more jovial side, kissing Ustinya Fyodorovna's hands despite her protests about their roughness and promising to perform a unique dance for them that evening. However, the visit ended disastrously the next day. Whether it was due to his overly enthusiastic dance or some offense he had caused, Ustinya Fyodorovna declared that he had treated her disrespectfully. As a result, he was thrown out of the flat. Despite being ejected, Zimoveykin managed to return several times, each time causing trouble until he finally wormed his way into Semyon Ivanovitch's confidence. Eventually, it was discovered that he had even stolen Semyon Ivanovitch's new trousers. Now, it seemed clear that Zimoveykin had played a role in leading Semyon Ivanovitch astray.

When Ustinya Fyodorovna learned that Semyon Ivanovitch was alive and well, her worries about his passport quickly disappeared, and she calmed down. Meanwhile, some of the other lodgers decided to prepare a humorous welcome for his return. They broke the bolt on his screen and rearranged his corner. They moved his well-guarded trunk to the foot of the bed and placed on the bed a dummy dressed in an old kerchief, cap, and mantle borrowed from the landlady. The figure looked so much like a real person that it could have been mistaken for one. When their prank was complete, they waited eagerly for Semyon Ivanovitch to come back, planning to tell him that his sister-in-law had arrived unexpectedly from the countryside and was now resting behind his screen.

However, they waited and waited, but Semyon Ivanovitch never returned.

As they waited, Mark Ivanovitch had already gambled away half a month's salary to Prepolovenko and Kantarev. Okeanov's nose had turned red and swollen from too many rounds of "flips on the nose" and "three cards." Avdotya, the servant, had nearly finished her sleep and twice thought of getting up to fetch firewood and light the stove. Meanwhile, Zinovy Prokofyevitch kept running outside every few minutes to check if Semyon Ivanovitch was on his way back, but all he achieved was soaking himself to the skin. Yet there was still no sign of Semyon Ivanovitch or the drunken vagabond. Eventually, everyone gave up and went to bed, leaving the makeshift "sister-in-law" hidden behind the screen, just in case.

It wasn't until four in the morning that a loud knock at the gate shattered the silence, making up for all the hours of waiting with its intensity. The noise woke everyone, and they rushed to find out who it was. To their shock, it was Semyon Ivanovitch—Mr. Prohartchin himself—but in such a terrible state that everyone gasped in alarm. The "sister-in-law" prank was completely forgotten. Semyon Ivanovitch was unconscious. A soaking wet, disheveled night-cabman had brought him back, carrying him like a bundle.

When Ustinya Fyodorovna demanded to know what had happened, the cabman replied, "He's not drunk. Not a drop of alcohol in him, I swear. But something seems to have happened—a fainting spell, a fit, or maybe someone struck him. Who knows?"

They propped Semyon Ivanovitch up against the stove to examine him more closely. It quickly became clear that he wasn't drunk, nor did he appear to have been physically assaulted. Instead, it seemed as though something deeper was wrong. He was unable to speak and was twitching as if in some kind of convulsion. His bewildered eyes blinked rapidly as he looked around at the group, all dressed in their nightclothes, trying to figure out what had happened.

The cabman, still standing by, explained further. "I picked him up out Kolomna way, from some folks—strange lot, not quite gentry but lively, jolly fellows. He was already in this state when they handed him over to me. Whether there had been a fight or it's just some sort of fit, I couldn't tell you. But they were having a good time, that's for sure."

Semyon Ivanovitch was carefully lifted by two or three strong men and carried to his bed. But as soon as he was placed down, he felt the "sister-in-law" figure on the bed and his sacred box beneath his feet. With a loud cry, he sprang up, squatting almost on his heels. Trembling violently, he frantically cleared a space around himself on the bed, using his hands and body to shove away anything in reach. His eyes darted around the room, filled with a mixture of fear and defiance. Despite his weakened state, there was a look of fierce determination in his trembling gaze, as if he were silently declaring that he would sooner die than let anyone lay a hand on even the smallest piece of his possessions.

Semyon Ivanovitch lay confined behind his screen for two or three days, completely cut off from the outside world and its petty concerns. By the next morning, everyone seemed to have forgotten about him, and time moved forward as usual. Hours blended into days, and the sick man, lost in a fog of fever and delirium, lay silently in bed. He neither groaned nor complained; instead, he remained still and subdued, as though hiding from the world like a hare pressing itself to the ground to avoid a hunter.

During the day, when the flat was quiet and the other lodgers were away at their offices, Semyon Ivanovitch would wake occasionally, his heavy thoughts drifting between awareness and exhaustion. He found some small comfort in the sounds of Ustinya Fyodorovna bustling about the kitchen or the soft shuffle of Avdotya's worn slippers as she moved through the rooms, sighing and muttering while cleaning. Time stretched endlessly, marked only by the slow, steady drip of water in the kitchen basin. Hours passed in drowsy monotony, heavy with silence and half-formed dreams.

Eventually, the lodgers would return, one by one or in groups. Their voices filled the air as they complained about the weather, declared their hunger, and laughed, argued, or played cards. Cups clinked as they prepared tea, and the noise of their activities seeped through the thin walls. At moments like these, Semyon Ivanovitch would stir, a half-formed thought urging him to join them at the tea table, as he was entitled to do. But the effort would prove too much, and he would sink back into his restless half-sleep. In his dreams, he imagined himself sitting with them, sipping tea and engaging in conversation. He even envisioned Zinovy Prokofyevitch introducing one of his nonsensical schemes about sisters-in-law. In these dreams, Semyon Ivanovitch would rise to defend himself, but a repeated phrase—"It has more than once been observed"—would silence him every time. Resigned, he would drift back into another dream, this time imagining it was the first of the month and he was receiving his salary at the office.

In this dream, he stood on the stairs, quickly unwrapping the paper from his money, glancing around nervously. He immediately hid half of his wages in his boot and began mentally dividing the rest. He planned to pay Ustinya Fyodorovna what he owed for board and lodging, buy a few necessities, and casually let it be known that his salary had been reduced, leaving nothing for his sister-in-law. He envisioned himself speaking with sympathy about her plight, ensuring his companions would remember her story for days, even weeks to come. In his dream, as he plotted this, Andrey Efimovitch, the perpetually silent clerk who had not spoken a word to him in twenty years, appeared on the stairs, counting his own money. The bald man shook his head solemnly and muttered, "Money! Without money, there's no porridge." As he turned to leave, he added grimly, "And I have seven children."

The dream took a darker turn as Semyon Ivanovitch suddenly felt accused. Though he knew he had no connection to Andrey's seven children, he felt an irrational guilt. Terrified, he imagined the bald man chasing him, demanding his salary and dismissing any claims from Semyon Ivanovitch's sister-in-law. Panicked, Semyon Ivanovitch ran, gasping for breath, accompanied by a crowd of people jingling coins in their pockets. The commotion carried him to a house fire he had seen before, amidst a throng of shouting spectators. In his fevered dream, Mr. Zimoveykin, the drunken cadger, reappeared and dragged him into the chaos. Flames roared, and familiar faces swirled around him: a giant man with enormous whiskers, a feeble old man with a milk can, and a shouting woman in rags, wailing about her children and lost coins.

As the dream reached its terrifying crescendo, Semyon Ivanovitch felt the crowd closing in on him. A singed peasant accused him of past wrongs, shouting accusations about an unpaid cab fare from years ago. The angry mob pressed closer, suffocating him. Semyon Ivanovitch tried to scream, but no sound came. At last, he woke with a start.

To his horror, he thought his bed and corner were engulfed in flames. The screen, the flat, and everything within it seemed to be burning—his bed, his pillow, his box, and even his precious mattress. He leapt up, clutching the mattress and dragging it behind him. Barefoot and in his shirt, he burst into Ustinya Fyodorovna's room, startling everyone. But it was not the flat that was on fire—only Semyon Ivanovitch's fevered imagination. He was promptly seized and carried back to his bed. It was as though he were a puppet being put away after a chaotic performance, packed back into a box alongside the other characters of his delirious dreams, waiting for the next act to begin.

All at once, everyone, young and old, gathered around Semyon Ivanovitch's bed, forming a line and fixing their curious, expectant eyes on him. Meanwhile, he began to regain consciousness but, whether out of shame or some other emotion, tried to pull the quilt over himself, as if to hide from the eager attention of his concerned visitors. Finally, Mark Ivanovitch broke the silence. Being a practical man, he began to speak in a friendly tone, encouraging Semyon Ivanovitch to stay calm. He said it was a shame to be lying ill like this, behaving almost like a child. Mark Ivanovitch joked that there were no official salaries for invalids and that their position, as far as he knew, didn't offer many advantages in the service.

It was clear that everyone truly cared about Semyon Ivanovitch and was trying to express sympathy. But despite their genuine concern, Semyon Ivanovitch responded with unexpected rudeness. He remained silent, stubbornly pulling the quilt higher and higher as though trying to disappear beneath it. Mark Ivanovitch, refusing to be put off, tried again to offer kind and comforting words, speaking in a soothing tone to suit the situation. However, Semyon Ivanovitch was unmoved. He muttered something unintelligible through clenched teeth and began to dart suspicious, hostile glances at the others, as though he wanted to reduce them to ashes with his eyes.

Seeing no progress, Mark Ivanovitch's patience wore thin. He noted the man's offense and obstinacy and, abandoning all gentleness, told him bluntly that it was time to get up. He declared it useless to keep lying there, shouting nonsensical things day and night about fires, sisters-in-law, drunken companions, locks, and boxes. Mark Ivanovitch scolded him for disturbing others' sleep and demanded that he stop behaving in such a ridiculous and degrading way. He asked him to consider others and bear this in mind going forward.

The words struck a nerve. Semyon Ivanovitch promptly turned toward Mark Ivanovitch, and in a hoarse but firm voice, he retorted, "You hold your tongue, you fool! You idle talker, you good-for-nothing! Do you think you're a prince? Do you even understand what I'm saying?"

Mark Ivanovitch, insulted but mindful of dealing with an ill man, managed to suppress his anger. Instead, he tried to reason with Semyon Ivanovitch and gently shame him out of his temper. But before he could get far, Semyon Ivanovitch interrupted with an indignant observation, declaring he would not tolerate anyone taking liberties with him, no matter how much poetry Mark Ivanovitch might write.

A brief silence followed this heated exchange. Then, recovering from his surprise, Mark Ivanovitch firmly but politely reminded Semyon Ivanovitch of his surroundings. "You must understand," he said, "that you are among gentlemen, and you ought to behave accordingly."

Mark Ivanovitch had a way of speaking that could impress a crowd when he chose to. However, Semyon Ivanovitch, unused to lengthy speeches and having spent years in relative silence, often struggled to express himself clearly. When he did attempt long sentences, one word seemed to lead to another, and so on, until the ideas tumbled out in a chaotic mess. This habit often caused him, despite his sensible nature, to say the most absurd things.

"You're lying," he declared now, his words sharp and disjointed. "You scoundrel! You good-for-nothing loafer! One day you'll be a beggar—you'll come crawling to me, you rascal. Take that, you so-called poet!"

To this outburst, Mark Ivanovitch could only respond with a mixture of irritation and exasperation. "Why, you're still raving, aren't you, Semyon Ivanovitch?" he muttered, shaking his head.

"I'll tell you this," said Semyon Ivanovitch. "Fools rave, drunkards rave, dogs rave, but a wise man acts sensibly. You don't even understand your own business, you loafer, you so-called educated man, you walking book! You'd catch fire and not even realize your head was burning. What do you think of that?"

"What... what do you mean, Semyon Ivanovitch? How would my head catch fire?" Mark Ivanovitch stammered, clearly puzzled.

Mark didn't press further, as it was obvious to everyone that Semyon Ivanovitch was still delirious and not in his right mind.

The landlady, however, couldn't resist adding her own commentary. She chimed in, saying that a house in Crooked Lane had burned down once because of a careless bald woman. This woman had lit a candle in the storage room and started the fire. But, the landlady assured everyone, such a thing would never happen in her flats.

"Enough of this nonsense!" Zinovy Prokofyevitch suddenly snapped, losing patience and cutting the landlady off. "You old crock, you silly man—are they teasing you again about your sister-in-law or those ridiculous dancing exams? Is that what this is about?"

"I'll tell you what," Semyon Ivanovitch barked, sitting upright in his bed and summoning all his fury for one last outburst. "Who's the fool here? You are! A dog's a fool, and so are you, you joking gentleman. But

I am not here to entertain you, sir. Do you hear me, puppy? I am not your servant!"

Semyon Ivanovitch seemed ready to say more, but he suddenly collapsed back onto his bed, utterly spent. His audience, who had been so eagerly watching, now stood in silence, utterly confused. They finally understood that something deeper was troubling Semyon Ivanovitch, but none of them knew how to approach the situation.

At that moment, the kitchen door creaked open, and the drunken vagrant, Mr. Zimoveykin, cautiously poked his head inside. He sniffed the air as though testing the atmosphere, a habit of his. It seemed as though everyone had been expecting him because they immediately waved him over, signaling him to come closer. Zimoveykin, clearly thrilled to be needed, hurried into the room and pushed his way to Semyon Ivanovitch's bedside.

Zimoveykin's appearance was a sight to behold. It was obvious he'd been through quite an ordeal during the night. The right side of his face was covered with a crude plaster; his swollen eyelids glistened as though from tears or irritation. His clothes were torn in several places, and the left side of his outfit was smeared with something unpleasant—likely mud from a puddle.

Under his arm, he carried a battered violin, which he had apparently been trying to sell.

Wasting no time, Zimoveykin addressed Semyon Ivanovitch with an air of authority, as though he fully understood the situation and had complete control over it. "What are you doing, Senka?" he said sternly. "Get up! What's this nonsense from a clever guy like you? Be sensible now, or I'll drag you out of that bed myself. Don't test me!"

This short but commanding speech stunned everyone in the room. They were even more surprised to see how Semyon Ivanovitch reacted. At the sight of Zimoveykin, he became visibly flustered, his confidence replaced with confusion and fear. He could barely manage to whisper a weak protest through clenched teeth.

"Go away, you scoundrel," Semyon Ivanovitch said. "You're a miserable creature—a thief! Do you hear me? Do you understand? You think you're something special, don't you? A real gentleman, a big shot!"

"No, my friend," Zimoveykin replied sharply, keeping his cool. "You've got it all wrong, my wise fellow, you old Prohartchin," he added, mocking Semyon Ivanovitch and glancing around with a smirk.

"Don't get all worked up! Behave yourself, Senka, or I'll spill everything—I'll tell them all about it, you hear?"

Semyon Ivanovitch clearly understood. He flinched at Zimoveykin's words, looking around desperately as if searching for a way out.

Zimoveykin, pleased with the reaction, was about to continue, but Mark Ivanovitch stepped in to calm things down. Once Semyon Ivanovitch seemed to settle, Mark began speaking in a measured tone, explaining to him that his fears were unfounded. He stressed that harboring such thoughts was not only unnecessary but also harmful and, worse yet, morally wrong. He added that Semyon Ivanovitch's behavior was setting a bad example and leading everyone else astray.

Everyone thought Mark's words might get through to Semyon Ivanovitch. By now, he was calmer and began to respond, though his answers didn't quite make sense. A quiet conversation followed. They asked him gently what he was so scared of, and though Semyon Ivanovitch replied, his answers were scattered and irrelevant. As the discussion continued, it spiraled into confusion. Soon, voices were raised, leading to shouting and even tears. Mark Ivanovitch eventually stormed off, red-faced, muttering that he'd never met anyone so stubborn. Oplevaniev spat in frustration, Okeanov looked alarmed, Zinovy Prokofyevitch grew teary-eyed, and Ustinya Fyodorovna began wailing that her lodger was losing his mind. She cried that he'd leave her without a passport and die somewhere, and she, a poor, lonely woman, would be left to deal with the fallout.

It became clear to everyone that their teasing had gone too far. Semyon Ivanovitch had overthought everything to the point of breaking down. Now, both he and his so-called friends were frightened by the mess they had created.

"What is it you're so afraid of?" Mark Ivanovitch yelled. "What's got you so rattled? Who even cares about you? Do you think anyone's out to get you? Who are you, anyway? You're nothing—a zero, a big fat nothing! What are you panicking about? Just because some woman got run over in the street, does that mean you'll get run over too? If a drunk lost his wallet, are your coat-tails in danger? A house burns down, and suddenly you think your head's going to catch fire? Is that it?"

"You... you idiot," Semyon Ivanovitch muttered. "If someone chopped off your nose, you'd eat it with bread and not even notice."

"Sure, I might be a dandy," Mark Ivanovitch shot back, ignoring the insult. "But I don't need to pass some exam to get married or learn to dance. My feet are planted firmly on the ground. What about you? Are you running out of space? Is the floor caving in under you or something?"

"Well, they won't ask you about it, will they? They'll just lock someone up, and that'll be the end of it," said one voice.

"The end of it? Is that what you think? What are you talking about now, huh?" came the reply.

"Why, they kicked out that drunken cadger, didn't they?"

"Yes, but that was a drunkard. You're a man, and so am I."

"Yes, I'm a man. But one day it's there, and the next day it's gone."

"Gone? What exactly do you mean by that?"

"I mean the office! The off—off—ice!"

"Yes, of course the office is important. It's needed," came a soothing reply.

"It's needed today, and it'll be needed tomorrow. But the day after that, it won't be needed anymore. Haven't you heard what happened?"

"Look, they'll pay you your salary for the year, you doubting fool, you man of little faith. And they'll find you another job because of your age."

"Salary? But what if I've already spent my salary? What if thieves come and steal my money? And I've got a sister-in-law, do you hear me? A sister-in-law!"

"A sister-in-law? You're still a man...."

"Yes, I am a man. But you, you're a well-read fool, do you hear? A battering ram, that's what you are! I'm not joking. Some jobs just disappear overnight, do you understand? And Demid—do you hear me?—Demid Vassilyevitch says the post will be done away with."

"Oh, enough with your Demid! You sinner, you know better...."

"In the blink of an eye, you'll lose your job, and then you'll have to make the best of it."

"You're raving! You've lost your mind! Tell us, what's really going on? Just admit it if you've done something wrong! There's no use in being ashamed. Are you out of your mind, my good man?"

"He's lost his mind! He's gone mad!" everyone cried out, wringing their hands in frustration. The landlady, fearing a fight, threw her arms around Mark Ivanovitch to stop him from attacking Semyon Ivanovitch.

"You heathen! You stubborn, heathen soul, you wise man!" Zimoveykin pleaded. "Senka, you're not someone who gets offended easily. You're polite, you're good-natured, do you hear me? All of this comes from your goodness. Look at me—I'm a fool, a beggar, but good people haven't abandoned me. They treat me with respect, and I'm thankful for that. Even the landlady here, she hasn't turned me away."

At this, Zimoveykin straightened himself and, with exaggerated formality, bowed low to the ground. "Here, see? I'm paying my respects to you, landlady!" he declared with a theatrical flourish.

After that, Semyon Ivanovitch would have kept talking, but this time they wouldn't let him. Everyone jumped in, pleading with him, assuring him, and trying to calm him down. They managed to make him feel thoroughly ashamed of himself. At last, in a weak voice, he asked for permission to explain.

"Fine then," he said. "I'm respectable, I'm quiet, I'm good, loyal, and devoted to the last drop of my blood, you know… Do you hear me, you puppy, you dandy? The job's going on, sure, but look—I'm poor. And what if they take it away? Do you hear me, you dandy? Shut up and try to understand! They'll take it, and that's the end of it. It's going on, and then suddenly it's not… Do you get it? And then I'll be left begging for bread. Do you hear?"

"Senka!" Zimoveykin shouted, his voice cutting through the growing commotion. "You're being rebellious! I'll report you! What are you even saying? Who do you think you are? Are you some kind of revolutionary, you dimwit? A rowdy fool they'd fire without hesitation. But who are you, really?"

"Well, that's just it," Semyon muttered.

"What?" Zimoveykin pressed.

"Well, there it is."

"What do you mean?" someone else chimed in.

"I mean, I'm free, he's free, and yet here I am lying down, thinking…"

"Thinking what?" someone asked.

"What if they say I'm rebellious?"

"Rebellious? Senka, rebellious!" Zimoveykin roared.

"Wait," Semyon Ivanovitch said, waving his hand to stop the escalating argument. "That's not what I mean. Try to understand, just try to understand, you fools. I'm law-abiding. I'm law-abiding today, I'll be law-abiding tomorrow, and then suddenly, out of nowhere, they'll throw me out and call me rebellious."

Mr. Prohartchin

"What nonsense are you talking about?" Mark Ivanovitch finally erupted, jumping up from his chair. He stormed over to the bed, shaking with frustration and anger. "What do you mean? You fool! You don't even own anything. Do you think the world revolves around you? Are you some kind of Napoleon? Who do you think you are? Tell me—are you a Napoleon?"

But Semyon Ivanovitch didn't answer. It wasn't that he was embarrassed by the comparison to Napoleon or afraid to take on such a title. He simply couldn't respond anymore. His illness had worsened. Tears suddenly streamed from his feverish, glassy eyes. He buried his burning head in his bony hands, which were frail from sickness. Sitting up in bed, he began to sob, confessing that he was poor, unlucky, foolish, and uneducated. He begged for forgiveness, for protection, for food and drink. He pleaded with them not to abandon him, his voice trembling with fear, as though he expected the walls to collapse around him.

Everyone's hearts softened with pity at the sight of him. The landlady, sobbing like a grieving peasant woman, gently laid him back in bed. Mark Ivanovitch, realizing there was no point in bringing up Napoleon again, softened as well and helped her. The others, wanting to do something useful, suggested giving him raspberry tea, claiming it would help immediately and

43

that Semyon would surely enjoy it. But Zimoveykin disagreed, insisting camomile tea or something similar would be better. Zinovy Prokofyevitch, feeling remorseful for having frightened Semyon Ivanovitch with silly ideas, began crying. Seeing that Semyon truly seemed destitute, Zinovy decided to start a collection among the tenants to help him.

Everyone was sighing and lamenting, overwhelmed with sympathy and grief. At the same time, they couldn't help but wonder how someone could become so completely consumed by fear. What was he so scared of? It would make sense if he had a prestigious job, a wife, or children, or if he were facing some kind of legal trouble. But he was just an insignificant man with nothing but a trunk and a German lock. He had spent over twenty years behind a screen, quietly saving his pennies, only to completely lose his mind over a casual comment.

"If only he realized," Okeanov later remarked, "that everyone struggles in life. If he'd just accept that, he wouldn't have panicked like this. He'd have kept his head, stopped acting out, and found a way to deal with it like the rest of us."

Throughout the entire day, the only topic of conversation was Semyon Ivanovitch. Everyone checked on him, asked about his condition, and tried their best to comfort him. But by evening, his state had worsened. He started muttering incoherently, feverish and delirious, slipping in and out of unconsciousness. The lodgers even considered calling a doctor. After a group discussion, they decided to watch over him throughout the night, taking turns to stay awake. They promised to wake the others immediately if anything unusual happened. To keep themselves from dozing off, they sat down to play cards, positioning Zimoveykin— the drunken cadger who had been lingering in the flat all day—beside Semyon Ivanovitch as a companion.

However, the card game quickly lost its appeal since it was played on credit and lacked any real excitement. Boredom took hold, leading to arguments, then loud disputes. Before long, everyone gave up the effort entirely, retreating to their own corners. Angry muttering and occasional shouts echoed in the flat for a while until, one by one, they fell asleep. Soon the entire place became silent, as quiet as an empty cellar. Adding to the eerie atmosphere, the flat was bitterly cold.

Okeanov was the last to succumb to sleep, hovering in a state between wakefulness and dreaming. As he later recounted, he thought he heard two men whispering nearby just before dawn. He believed one of the voices belonged to Zimoveykin, who seemed to be waking up his friend Remnev. According to Okeanov, the two whispered for a while before Zimoveykin got up and tried to unlock the kitchen door. Later, the landlady insisted the key—usually kept under her pillow—had mysteriously gone missing that night. Okeanov also claimed to have heard the pair moving behind Semyon Ivanovitch's screen, lighting a candle there. After that, he knew nothing more, having finally drifted off.

Suddenly, a blood-curdling scream tore through the flat, jolting everyone awake. The sound seemed to come from behind Semyon Ivanovitch's screen, and for a moment, many thought they saw the faint flicker of a candle going out. Panic erupted as everyone leapt from their beds and rushed toward the source of the noise. Chaos ensued—a scuffle broke out, accompanied by shouting, cursing, and wild accusations. When someone managed to strike a light, they found Zimoveykin and Remnev locked in a violent struggle, yelling insults at one another. Zimoveykin was shouting, "It wasn't me! This scoundrel did it!" while Remnev countered, "Don't touch me! I swear I'm innocent!" Both looked utterly disheveled and barely human in their rage and fear.

However, the real shock came when they noticed that Semyon Ivanovitch was no longer in his bed. They parted the two fighters and dragged them aside, peering behind the screen. There, under the bed, they found Semyon Ivanovitch. Somehow, in his unconscious state, he had slipped off the mattress, pulling the quilt and pillow with him. His bed was now stripped bare except for the greasy old mattress he had always used. They gently pulled him out and laid him back on the bed, but it quickly became apparent that their efforts were in vain. Semyon Ivanovitch was gone. His body was stiff, and his limbs lifeless.

The group stood in stunned silence, staring at the lifeless figure. Semyon Ivanovitch twitched faintly, his body shuddering as if making one last attempt to move. His eyes blinked weakly, resembling the way severed heads were said to blink moments after an execution. Then, gradually, even these faint movements ceased. His body lay still, and the room seemed to grow quieter. Semyon Ivanovitch had passed, taking his secrets and sorrows with him.

Speculation filled the room. Some wondered if he had been frightened to death by a dream, as Remnev later suggested. Others suspected foul play or some unknown tragedy. But no one could say for certain. It seemed that even the most extraordinary events—a sudden dismissal, an unexpected reward, or even a house fire—would have failed to rouse Semyon Ivanovitch at that moment.

While the initial shock wore off and everyone regained their composure, the flat descended into chaos. The landlady, Ustinya Fyodorovna, began rummaging through Semyon Ivanovitch's belongings. She dragged out his box from under the bed, rifled through his mattress, and even searched his boots, all while muttering in a frantic flurry. The lodgers, meanwhile, bombarded Remnev and Zimoveykin with questions, demanding answers. Amid the uproar, Okeanov—usually the quietest and most unassuming of the group—took advantage of the confusion. Grabbing his hat, he slipped out unnoticed.

As the disorder reached its peak, the door suddenly opened, and a severe-looking man entered, followed by Yaroslav Ilyitch, several subordinates, and, at the back of the group, a sheepish-looking Okeanov. The stern gentleman examined Semyon Ivanovitch's body briefly, announced that the man was indeed deceased (a fact everyone already knew), and compared the situation to another recent case of sudden death. Then, with a shrug, he declared the disturbance unnecessary and left.

Yaroslav Ilyitch took charge, questioning the lodgers and confiscating Semyon Ivanovitch's box, which the landlady had been trying to pry open. He ordered the scattered belongings to be returned to their places, commenting on the state of Semyon Ivanovitch's boots, which were so worn they were practically useless. Finally, he demanded the key to the box, which was found in Zimoveykin's pocket. Opening it ceremoniously, he revealed its contents: scraps of fabric, old soles, buttons, and other odds and ends, all of little value. The only item of worth was the German lock.

The investigation shifted to the mattress, which someone suggested cutting open. As they lifted it, a clinking sound drew their attention. A small, paper-wrapped bundle had fallen out, revealing a dozen roubles. Further inspection uncovered a slit in the mattress, its edges fresh from a knife. Inside, they found more bundles of money, along with a knife hastily shoved into the stuffing. Roubles, coins, and even an old five-kopeck piece tumbled out as they continued their search. Finally, someone called for scissors to dismantle the entire mattress.

The dim, flickering candle cast a wavering light over a scene that would have been fascinating to any outside observer. About a dozen lodgers crowded around Semyon Ivanovitch's bed, each draped in a mishmash of nightclothes, their appearances as unkempt as their moods. Hair unbrushed, faces unshaven, and sleep still clinging to their eyes, they presented a motley group. Some faces were pale, beads of sweat glistening on foreheads, while others were flushed with feverish anxiety or shivering from the cold. The landlady stood silently at the edge of the group, her hands folded in front of her, her expression a mix of shock and resignation, as if awaiting Yaroslav Ilyitch's instructions. Above them, from the warm perch of the stove, the servant Avdotya and the landlady's favorite cat peered down with a mix of curiosity and fright.

The small flat was in disarray. The broken screen lay discarded on the floor, the disheveled quilt and pillow were strewn about, dotted with fluff and feathers from the mattress, and the battered wooden table held a steadily growing pile of coins gleaming in the candlelight. Meanwhile, Semyon Ivanovitch remained undisturbed, lying stiffly on the bed as if he were oblivious to the chaos around him.

When the scissors were finally fetched, Yaroslav Ilyitch's assistant took it upon himself to shake the mattress vigorously in an attempt to free it from under Semyon Ivanovitch's back. Ever polite, Semyon Ivanovitch shifted slightly to make room, rolling onto his side. A second shake prompted him to turn onto his face, but when the assistant gave the mattress another forceful tug, Semyon Ivanovitch, unbalanced by the movement, suddenly slipped through the gap left by a missing slat in the bed frame. His head vanished under the bed, leaving only his thin, bony legs sticking straight up, blue and motionless, like the charred branches of a tree.

This awkward position immediately aroused suspicion. Zinovy Prokofyevitch, ever curious, led the charge to investigate what might be hidden under the bed. Several lodgers crawled beneath, bumping heads in their haste, but they found nothing of interest. Yaroslav Ilyitch barked at them to release Semyon Ivanovitch, and two of the more level-headed lodgers took hold of his legs and dragged him back into the light. They laid him across the bed, his usual composure now somewhat ruffled.

As the mattress was cut open, tufts of hair and flock flew about the room, while the growing pile of coins on the table began to take on an astonishing scale. The assortment was remarkable: solid silver roubles, sturdy one-and-a-half rouble coins, elegant half-rouble pieces, and smaller denominations such as twenty-kopeck coins and even tarnished five-kopeck pieces. Each was carefully wrapped in paper, sorted with a methodical precision that hinted at Semyon Ivanovitch's meticulous nature. Among the hoard were rare finds:

German kreutzers, old coins from the reigns of Peter and Catherine, and a Napoleon d'or. There were even copper coins, though these were heavily corroded. The single red banknote they discovered seemed almost insignificant amidst the glittering treasure.

When the mattress yielded no further surprises, it was shaken one last time for good measure. The coins were stacked on the table and counted meticulously. At first glance, the sheer volume of money suggested an enormous fortune, but the final total came to exactly 2,497 roubles and fifty kopecks. If Zinovy Prokofyevitch's proposed subscription from the day before had been collected, the amount would likely have rounded up to a neat 2,500 roubles.

The lodgers stood dumbfounded. The landlady, though clearly disheartened by the discovery, wailed dramatically, lamenting the betrayal of her trust. Yaroslav Ilyitch, ever methodical, took charge. He sealed Semyon Ivanovitch's box, listened impatiently to the landlady's complaints about unpaid rent, and advised her on how to file an official claim. A receipt was issued for the money, and inquiries about the mythical sister-in-law were quietly dropped after the group collectively agreed that she was likely a figment of Semyon Ivanovitch's imagination.

As the initial shock subsided, the mood in the room shifted. The lodgers began exchanging suspicious glances, each silently reassessing their late companion. For some, the revelation of Semyon Ivanovitch's hidden fortune felt like a personal affront. How had he managed to save so much while living among them in such apparent poverty? Mark Ivanovitch, trying to maintain his usual composure, attempted to explain the deceased's sudden panic, but his words fell on deaf ears. Zinovy Prokofyevitch stood lost in thought, while Okeanov, slightly tipsy, seemed unusually introspective. Kantarev, a small man with a sharp nose, quietly packed his belongings and announced his departure, citing the high cost of living as his reason.

The landlady, meanwhile, alternated between sobbing and cursing Semyon Ivanovitch for taking advantage of her kindness. When someone asked why he hadn't placed his savings in a bank, Mark Ivanovitch offered a simple answer: "He lacked imagination, my dear. Too simple for such things."

And so the flat returned to its peculiar version of normalcy, the absence of Semyon Ivanovitch leaving a lingering unease among those he had left behind.

"Yes, and you've been just as simple-minded, my dear woman," Okeanov added with a shake of his head.

"For twenty years, the man stayed hidden away here in your flat, barely making a sound, and now he's been knocked down by a mere feather—while you busied yourself cooking cabbage soup and never noticed a thing. Ah, what a shame, my dear woman!"

"Oh, the poor soul," the landlady lamented, wringing her hands. "Why would he need a bank? If only he had come to me and said, 'Ustinyushka, my dear, take this, all I have. Keep it for me and care for me in my old age while I'm still alive.' I swear on the holy ikon, I would have fed him, given him drink, looked after him like my own child. But no—ah, the sinner, the deceiver! He tricked me, lied to me, a poor, helpless woman!"

They turned back to the bed where Semyon Ivanovitch now lay, dressed in his best—and only—suit. His stiff chin was awkwardly hidden behind a hastily tied cravat. Though his face was washed and his hair brushed, he wasn't quite shaven, as there was no razor in the flat. Zinovy Prokofyevitch's razor, dull for over a year, had been sold off long ago at Tolkutchy Market, and the others made do with visits to the barber.

The room was still in disarray. The broken screen, which had once shielded Semyon Ivanovitch's modest corner, lay crumpled on the floor, now exposing his private world to all. It stood as a fitting metaphor: death, with its unyielding hand, had stripped away the veil of secrecy, laying bare the little schemes, the quiet hoards, and the peculiar habits he had hidden. Stuffing from the mattress was strewn about in messy piles, and the room itself, suddenly hushed, might have inspired a poet to liken it to the shattered nest of a swallow—destroyed by a storm, the tiny nestlings lost, their once-warm sanctuary of feathers and fluff scattered all around.

Yet, in his repose, Semyon Ivanovitch bore little resemblance to a mournful bird. Instead, he seemed more like a cunning, aging sparrow—sharp-eyed, defiant even in death. He lay utterly still now, unmoved by the sobs and laments of his heartbroken landlady. His face, however, suggested something altogether different. It was as though, even in death, he was deep in thought, calculating, planning. His lips were pursed tightly, with a sharpness none had seen in him before. He seemed, strangely, wiser now—his right eye subtly squinted, as if appraising some invisible ledger or pondering a shrewd strategy. It was almost as though Semyon Ivanovitch had a message to deliver, something important to explain before it was too late.

And for a moment, it felt as though his voice could be heard, clear and deliberate in the silence.

"What's this nonsense? Stop it already, you silly woman. Stop whining! Go to bed, sleep it off, do you hear me? I'm dead now—what's the use of all this fuss? Enough! Really, it's not so bad lying here. Though... hold on. That's not what I meant. You see, you're a fine lady, a very fine lady, and I'm just saying, hypothetically, what if I'm not dead? What if—just think about it—I get up? What then, huh? What would you do?"

It was as though the room held its breath, waiting for an answer to the unspoken question, for some resolution to the quiet mystery that had been Semyon Ivanovitch's life.

Thank You for Reading

Dear Reader,

We hope this timeless classic has sparked your imagination and enriched your literary journey. Now that you've turned the final page, we want to share a vision for the future of reading—one where every classic you've ever wanted to explore is at your fingertips, in a format that best suits your life.

We'd like to invite you to gain immediate, unlimited digital & audiobook access to hundreds of the most treasured literary classics ever written—along with the option to secure deluxe paperback, hardcover & box set editions at printing cost. Together, we can spark a new global literary renaissance alongside our small, independent publishing house called "The Library of Alexandria."

Thousands of years ago, the Library of Alexandria stood as a beacon of knowledge—until it was lost to history. We aim to reignite that spirit of preservation and discovery right now, in the modern age—only this time, it's accessible to all, in every language and every format.

Picture a world where every timeless classic, novel, poem, or philosophical treatise is not only available to read but also updated for today's readers—modernized, translated into any language or dialect, and ready to enjoy in any format you choose, whether that is in an eBook, audiobook, paperback, or deluxe hardcover & box set version a printing cost.

By joining our movement to rebuild the modern Library of Alexandria, you become part of an unprecedented mission to offer:

Unlimited Audiobook & eBook Access to the Greatest Classics of All Time

Instantly explore thousands of legendary works, from Plato and Shakespeare to Jane Austen and Leo Tolstoy. All are instantly ready to read or listen to, giving you a complete literary universe at your fingertips.

Paperback & Deluxe Editions at Printing Costs:

Purchase any title in a paperback, deluxe hardbound, or deluxe boxset edition at printing costs, shipped right to your doorstep. Curate your personal library of Alexandria with editions worthy of display—crafted to last, designed to captivate, and delivered straight to your door.

Modern translations for Contemporary Readers in all languages and dialects

Discover a vast selection of classics reimagined in clear, current language—no more struggling with outdated phrases or obscure references. Next to the original versions, we aim to offer translations in as many languages and dialects as possible.

As we continue our translation efforts and add new languages, readers everywhere can connect with these works as if they were written today. By bridging linguistic divides, you're contributing to ensuring that these timeless stories become more meaningful, accessible, and inspiring for people across the globe.

Your Personal Library of Alexandria:

Over the months and years, you'll curate a unique physical archive of classics—each volume a testament to your taste, curiosity, and love of knowledge. It's not just about owning books—it's about curating a cultural legacy you'll cherish and pass down for generations to come.

Join a Global Literary Renaissance:

Your support fuels an ongoing mission: allowing us to reinvest in offering deluxe print editions (including special boxsets) at their true cost, broaden the range of available formats and translations, and extend the reach of these works to new audiences worldwide. By joining today, you're not just preserving a legacy of masterpieces; you set in motion a powerful wave of literary accessibility.

We are more than a publisher—we're a movement, and we can't do it alone. Your support lets us scale our mission, preserving and reimagining history's greatest works for tomorrow's readers.

Become a Torchbearer of knowledge.

Thank you for picking up this book and allowing us into your literary journey. As you turn the pages, know that you're part of something larger: a global effort to keep these stories alive, share their wisdom across borders and generations, and spark a true cultural revival for the modern era.

If this resonates with you—please consider taking the next step by visiting:

www.libraryofalexandria.com

With gratitude and a shared love of knowledge,

The Modern Library of Alexandria Team

Visit:

www.libraryofalexandria.com

Or scan the code below:

www.ingramcontent.com/pod-product-compliance
Lightning Source LLC
Chambersburg PA
CBHW011525240626
47154CB00009B/2978

* 9 7 8 1 8 0 4 2 1 9 0 5 8 *